SHOW

by

ANNE FINE

Illustrated by Valerie Littlewood

HAMISH HAMILTON LTD
LONDON

For My Cordelia

Published by the Penguin Group
27 Wrights Lane, London W8 5TZ, England
Penguin Books USA Inc., 375 Hudson Street, New York, New York 10014, USA
Penguin Books Australia Ltd, Ringwood, Victoria, Australia
Penguin Books Canada Ltd, 10 Alcorn Avenue, Toronto, Ontario, Canada M4V 3B2
Penguin Books (NZ) Ltd, 182–190 Wairau Road, Auckland 10, New Zealand

Penguin Books Ltd, Registered Offices: Harmondsworth, Middlesex, England

First published in Great Britain 1990 by Hamish Hamilton Ltd

Text copyright © 1990 by Anne Fine
Illustrations copyright © 1990 by Valerie Littlewood
3 5 7 9 10 8 6 4

The moral rights of the author and artist have been asserted

British Library Cataloguing in Publication Data
CIP data for this book is available from the British Library

ISBN 0-241-12906-0

Set in 15pt Baskerville by Rowland Phototypesetting Ltd
Bury St Edmunds, Suffolk
Printed and bound in Great Britain by
Butler & Tanner Ltd, Frome and London

Chapter One

Miss Henry said, "On Monday, I want every single person in the class to give a little show."

"Everyone?"

"Give a little show?"

"What sort of show?"

"Any sort of show," said Miss Henry. "I'm sure everyone in this room can do something. You could sing a song, or do a dance, or show us some acrobatics. Or you could give a little five-minute speech about your pet, or what you did in the holidays."

She picked up the chalk.

"I'm going to write everyone's name on the blackboard," she said. "When you have given us your little show, I'll rub it out."

Anna watched as Miss Henry's stick of chalk squeaked its way across the blackboard, writing up names: Philip, Asha, Laura, James, Stephen, Talitha, Anna!

There it was, then. In black and white. No chance of getting out of

giving a show unless she crept back into the classroom after school, and rubbed it off herself.

But that would leave a gap in all the names, because Miss Henry was just carrying on: William, Moira, Rohan, Suzie, Arif...

So many of them! What would everyone do? They weren't circus children. They weren't at an acting school. They were just perfectly normal. What sort of show could they give? What would they do?

Anna followed everyone out of the classroom. They were all chatting excitedly. Everyone seemed to be bursting with ideas.

"I'm going to borrow my uncle's

four savage guard dogs, and show everybody how they attack strangers."

"Don't be so silly, Philip. He wouldn't lend them to you. And Miss Henry wouldn't let them into the school."

"I'm going to show everyone my diving."

"Don't be so silly, Laura. We don't have a swimming-pool."

"I'm going to show everyone how my mother makes fancy wedding dresses for the clothes shop on the corner."

"Don't be so silly, Asha. Five minutes, she said. A fancy wedding dress takes *hours* to make."

They were still talking about it all the way over the playground. Anna

4

tagged along behind, still listening.

"I'm going to show how you make a clay pot, and fire it and paint it and glaze it."

"Don't be so silly, James. Clay pots take weeks to finish."

"I'm going to teach everyone how to dance a Scottish reel."

"Don't be so silly, Moira. We'd have to move all the tables out of the classroom."

"I'm going to get my grandfather to teach me how to charm a snake."

"Don't be so silly, Rohan. You haven't got a snake. You haven't even got a magic pipe. And this isn't India, so it probably wouldn't work."

They were still chattering about the shows at the school gates.

"What are you going to do?"

"Not telling."

"Please. Pretty, pretty please."

"No."

"Meanie beanie!"

"No."

And poor little Anna was still listening.

That's how she felt – *poor little Anna*. Most of the time she fitted in. Nobody noticed her. She wasn't tall and confident, like Talitha. She wasn't clever and funny, like Suzie. She didn't wear wonderful new clothes, like Moira. She couldn't do cartwheels and backflips, like Laura. But she just rubbed along. She didn't have a really good best friend. But, on the other hand, she didn't have any enemies either. She didn't mind going to school in the mornings. But she was really glad when the bell rang at the end of the day, and she was allowed to go home.

There was absolutely nothing special about Anna at all, and she couldn't do anything special.

So what on earth was she going to do to get her name rubbed safely off the blackboard? What could she think of doing for her show?

Nothing. Nothing at all.

Chapter Two

Anna walked home in a daze. She had just one weekend – just two whole days – to think of a good show.

It was hopeless. And asking her mother didn't help much. Each time her mother thought of something she could do, Anna was sure she couldn't.

"Sing a song," Mum suggested.

"I can't sing."

"Recite a poem."

"I'd be so scared, I'd get the words mixed up."

8

Her little brother tried to help as well. "Tell a joke."

"No one would laugh at it. They'd laugh at *me*."

"Take Scruff, then. Do a puppet-show."

Simon was crazy about puppet-shows. He'd always loved them, ever since he was a baby. Every single night he made Anna slip Scruff, their rabbit puppet, on her hand and give him a private show over the edge of their bunk-beds.

"Good evening," Anna would say in Scruff's funny little rabbit voice.

"Good evening!" Simon would chant back enthusiastically.

And then, while Simon giggled, Anna would make Scruff sing a little song, or tell a joke, or do a magic trick. And whatever it was, Simon loved it. So maybe her brother was right. Maybe she *could* do something after all.

Anna slid off her chair and went into the bedroom. She found poor Scruff hanging over the top bar of the bunk-beds. He didn't look tidy and he didn't look comfortable. Anna picked him up and slid his furry body on her hand. His long ears drooped.

"Hello, Scruff," she said to him,

and wiggled his ears in a greeting.

"Hi, Anna," said Scruff in his peculiar little rabbit voice. "Want to hear a good joke?"

"Yes, please," said Anna.

"What do you get if you pour fresh tea down a rabbit hole?"

Anna cocked her head to one side and looked puzzled.

"I don't know, Scruff," she said. "What *do* you get if you pour fresh tea down a rabbit hole?"

"Hot cross bunnies!" said Scruff. He laughed so hard his ears flapped right round his head, practically blinding him.

"That's very good," said Simon. He was watching from the door. "They'll all like that."

But Anna wasn't at all convinced.

"No, they won't," she said gloomily. "They'll think it's stupid because they can see my lips moving. I can't make Scruff talk without moving my lips. I'm not a trained ventriloquist!"

She sounded so worried and cross that Simon tried to comfort her.

"It won't matter if your lips move," he said. "Everyone knows that Scruff's only a puppet."

"That's right!" snapped Anna. "And that's what will make it such a

rotten show!"

She peeled Scruff off her hand, and hurled him fiercely across the room. He ended up landing upside down in her schoolbag. He looked even more untidy and uncomfortable than he had looked hanging on the bars of the bed, but Anna didn't care.

"I'll think of something else," she announced. "I have two whole days. I'm bound to think of something."

But one whole day went by, and poor Anna thought of nothing at all. Well, that's not true, exactly. She thought of dozens of things. She thought of saying a nursery rhyme backwards, or standing on her head, or showing everyone how to grow mustard and cress on a damp flannel. But they might not recognise the nursery rhyme at all, even forwards. And she couldn't bear the thought of standing on her head in front of everyone and then toppling over. And there wasn't any time to grow mustard and cress.

By the time Granny came round on

Sunday, Anna was desperate. And then she suddenly had an idea.

"Granny, would you show me how to knit a scarf?"

Winter was coming. They'd all want to know how to knit a woolly scarf.

Granny was delighted.

"Of course, dear. Fetch me the knitting needles. And the wool."

Knitting needles? Wool? Oh, why oh why hadn't she thought of this yesterday, when all the shops were open?

Anna burst into tears.

Chapter Three

Granny and Mum did their best.
They always did. Granny sent Simon
down to the Chinese take-away to
borrow a pair of chopsticks. Then
Mum sent him next door to ask their
neighbour for the cork off an old wine
bottle. They cut the cork in half and
twisted a bit onto the end of each
plastic chopstick. Then Granny sent
everyone looking for wool.

They couldn't find much. And
what they did find was all short little

16

strands, and different colours. You couldn't knit a scarf with that.

"We'll knit a dolly's scarf, then," said Granny.

Anna was too miserable to argue. She knew it was a waste of time. Probably none of the class still played with dolls, and, if they did, they probably wouldn't admit it in front of everyone else. She couldn't give a show, teaching them how to knit a doll's scarf.

But there was no point in upsetting Granny.

So Anna sat on a stool by Granny's chair, and learned to wrap the wool the right way round her plastic chopsticks, and make her stitches, and knit her rows. Whenever the

colour she was using ran out, Granny
knotted on another, and they carried
on. It was a very bright and colourful
scarf – and very, very thin. Only ten
stitches wide. Just right for a doll. No
use for a show.

And, as soon as Granny had gone,
poor Anna stuffed the stupid little
doll's scarf away, out of sight, at the

bottom of her schoolbag, so she
wouldn't even have to look at it as
she got ready for bed.

It was about the worst night of
Anna's life. She cried so hard she got
a damp patch on her pillow, and on her
nightie, and on Mum's nightie when
she came in to cuddle her. She cried
so hard that Simon couldn't sleep,
and had to be carried, wrapped up in
his downie, into the other room, onto
the sofa. She cried so hard her mother
ran out of paper tissues.

And out of patience.

"For heaven's sake!" she said to
Anna. "It's only a show!"

"Only a show!" howled Anna.
"Only a show!" Her eyes were red-
rimmed and her hair was stuck to her

cheeks with salty, dried-up tears.

"That's right," her mother said. "Only a show. And you will think of something. You are as lively, and do as many interesting things, as everyone else."

Was she? Did she? Anna thought about it as she lay quietly in her mother's arms, her sobbing fit over. She didn't think she could do anything much. But Mum thought she was special. And so did Granny. And Simon thought her puppet-shows were brilliant. She only had to slide Scruff onto her hand ... and put on her funny rabbit voice ... and tell a joke...

She couldn't think any further. She was asleep at last.

By the time morning came, Anna was
in a very different mood.

"Want to stay home?" asked her
mother.

"No," Anna said. "For heaven's
sake. It's only a show."

Simon peered at his sister
curiously. She looked a bit pale and
her eyes were still a little swollen from
crying. But she looked calm enough.

"What are you going to do?" he
asked.

"I don't know," Anna said. "And I
don't care."

"That's right," Simon agreed. "It's
only a show."

Chapter Four

They started straight after register.
Everyone seemed keen.

When Miss Henry asked, "Who
wants to be first?" half the class shot
their hands up in the air. Maybe they
really did want to perform their little
shows. Maybe they just wanted to get
the horror and nervousness of it all
over, and have their names rubbed
safely off the blackboard. Anna
wasn't sure. But it certainly looked
as if she would be left alone, if she

wanted, till the very end.

Then, when everyone else had finished, she could get up and give a little five-minute speech about what she did in the holidays. It would be very boring. She hadn't done much. All that she did was teach Simon how to ride a two-wheeler bike, and watch Mum paint their bedroom a nicer blue, and she had gone to stay with Dad for a few days. But nothing exciting. Everyone would get very bored, listening. But it would only last five minutes. And then it would be over.

And, for heaven's sake, it was only a show.

Everyone else was brilliant. Asha went first. She couldn't show them

how her mother made fancy wedding
dresses for the shop on the corner. She
didn't have time. So instead she
showed them how to make a dress out
of black, shiny, plastic dustbin-liners.
She showed them how to cut the
bags up, and where to staple them
together, or stick the sellotape. And
soon she was standing in front of them
in a posh, slinky, glossy black dress,

and they were all cheering and clapping.

"Brilliant!" "Wonderful!" "Well done, Asha!"

Miss Henry beamed, and rubbed Asha's name off the blackboard.

"Who's next?"

Laura ran out to the front. She peeled off her jeans and her sweater, and underneath she was wearing her purple leotard with the glittering stars.

"I wanted to show you my diving," she said. "But we don't have a pool. So I'm going to show you ten yoga postures, a cartwheel and a backflip. And then I'm going to finish up by standing on my head. That's when you clap."

25

And, sure enough, when she'd done her ten yoga postures, her cartwheel and her backflip, and finished up standing on her head with her toes pointing elegantly toward the ceiling, that's when everyone clapped.

"Terrific!" "Amazing!" "Really sensational, Laura!"

Her name was rubbed off the blackboard as everyone cheered.

"Who's next?"

James wanted to go next. He didn't have time to show them how to make a clay pot, and fire it and paint it and glaze it. So he just showed them how to make potato sculptures.

"Take an old potato," he told them. "Cut off the bottom so it will stand up on the table. Then carve a face on it."

26

They watched, fascinated, as he poked out eyes, and ears, and a nose and a mouth, and even carved a little broken tooth. When he had finished, he pulled one he'd done weeks before out of his pocket.

"Look," he said. "This has been drying out by our hot-water tank for a whole month, so it's finished."

It looked revolting, like a real shrunken head. Everyone cheered and stamped.

"Terrific!" "Fabulous!" "Good old James!"

Proudly, James rubbed his own name off the blackboard.

One by one, everyone did their show. Moira didn't have the space to teach them Scottish reels, so instead she taught them all how to do a perfect curtsey, in case they ever met the Queen. Rohan hadn't found a snake or a magic pipe, so instead of snake charming, he showed them a couple of tricks with playing cards. William said afterwards that he could see extra cards up Rohan's sleeve all the time, but no one heard because of the clapping and cheering.

"Magic!" "Amazing!" "Clever Rohan!"

Their names were rubbed off the board.

Talitha showed them how to wear a sari. Philip gave a little talk about his cat and his goldfish. Suzie told three jokes and forgot the end of the fourth, but nobody minded. They all cheered just the same.

Stephen sang a sea-shanty his stepfather had taught him. Nicola showed them how to braid long hair into a crocodile-plait. Arif rattled off a poem in French.

Their names were rubbed off the blackboard.

And that left Anna.

Chapter Five

Anna had told herself a hundred
times that it didn't matter – it was
only a show – but she certainly felt
nervous. So nervous that, as she
stood up, she clumsily knocked her
schoolbag with her elbow, toppling it
off the table onto the floor. All the
things in it fell out, including Scruff
the rabbit and the long, brightly-
coloured doll's scarf.

Philip pounced on Scruff, and
picked him up.

"Oh, good! A rabbit puppet! Anna's going to do a puppet-show! I *love* puppets."

Everyone cheered in advance.

Suzie snatched up the brightly-coloured doll's scarf. "Look! Anna's rabbit has his own scarf!"

Everyone kept cheering.

"Come on, Anna! Hurry up. Start the show!"

What could poor Anna do? If they were all sitting there expecting a puppet-show, she couldn't just give them a boring five-minute talk about teaching Simon how to ride a two-wheeler, and watching Mum paint her bedroom.

Could she?

No.

Anna walked to the front of the class. Terrified, she looked round at the sea of grinning faces.

"Good morning, everyone," she said, extremely softly and nervously.

"Good morning!" they all chanted back, as loudly and enthusiastically as Simon always chanted back "Good evening!" when she did one of her little bedtime shows. So it seemed almost easy to say the next thing a little bit louder.

"I'd like to introduce to you my rabbit, Mr Scruff."

"Good morning, Mr Scruff," everyone chanted.

"Good morning, children," said Mr Scruff. Anna's lips moved, but only a little. And nobody seemed to notice, anyway – any more than they noticed the staples in Asha's glossy black dress, or the wobbles when

Laura did her yoga. And it was a really good rabbit voice. Simon always said so.

"Scruff here," said Anna, "may not look up to much, being quite tatty and old, but he has great magic and mystical powers which we are going to demonstrate to you this morning."

(She nearly said 'tonight' because of Simon; but she managed to stop herself just in time.)

She held the scarf out towards the front row.

"May I have a volunteer to blindfold the rabbit?"

Talitha rushed forward. Anna watched her make a neat job of blindfolding Scruff with the doll's scarf, tying a proper knot behind

Anna's fingers, and even managed to smile at her when she had finished. Then:

"This rabbit cannot see anything at all now," Anna confidently announced.

She held up three fingers on her other hand.

"Rabbit. How many fingers am I holding up?"

"I can't tell you," said Scruff. "Because, now I've been blind-folded, I can't see anything at all. Everything's gone dark."

Anna turned to her audience. To her astonishment, they were already giggling like Simon always did.

"He cannot see a thing," she carried on. "But he will demonstrate

his magic and mystical powers. Can I
have another volunteer to place an
object – any object at all – on the
table in front of Scruff? His long,
experienced ears will pick up the
magic vibrations. And he will tell
you what the object is."

"Impossible!" someone shouted out
from the back. "I won't believe it till I

see it!"

Suzie put the orange she'd brought to school for her snack on the table in front of Scruff.

"Rabbit," ordered Anna. "Use your magic and mystical powers."

Scruff turned his head from side to side. He flapped his ears. He sniffed the wind.

"It is an orange," he declared.

Everyone cheered wildly. Anna grinned.

"Again!" "Maybe he peeped!" "Check the blindfold!"

Anna looked serious. She asked Arif to check the blindfold. And then she watched as he took his plastic skeleton keyring out of his pocket and laid it on the desk in front of Scruff.

"Try that," Arif challenged Scruff.

Scruff flapped his ears. He sniffed the wind. He turned his head from side to side.

"It is a plastic skeleton keyring," he announced.

"Extraordinary!" "Unbelievable!" "Magic!"

But someone at the back called out, "He must be *cheating* somehow. Try something else!"

While everyone cheered, James slid

a five pence coin onto the table.

Scruff sniffed the wind. He turned his head from side to side. He flapped his ears.

"It is a five pence coin," he finally announced.

"Fantastic!" "Brilliant!" "How does he *do* it?"

"Do it again!"

Anna was perfectly ready to do it again. In fact, she was perfectly happy. Left to herself, she would have carried on forever. They were a better audience even than Simon. But, tragically, her five minutes were over, and Miss Henry stepped forward with her board-rubber in her hand, and swiftly rubbed Anna's name off the blackboard. Anna felt real disappointment, seeing it go.

"That's it!" Miss Henry said. "Show's over. Mustn't tire the poor rabbit."

Anna peeled the doll's scarf off Scruff's head, and made him take a bow. There was more cheering.

"Amazing!"

"Brilliant!"

"Wonderful!"

She bowed herself, several times, grinning hugely – until Miss Henry gently took her arm, and steered her back to her place at the table.

Only a show, indeed! Why, it was a triumph!